CHOOSE
YOUR
TRUTH

JO MILES

Cover design copyright © 2023 by Niki Lenhart
nikilen-designs.com

Published by Water Dragon Publishing
waterdragonpublishing.com

ISBN 978-1-959804-31-4 (Trade Paperback)

10 9 8 7 6 5 4 3 2 1

AUTHOR'S NOTE

This story is for all the warrior-journalists and misinformation-fighters out there. Keep doing what you're doing. The world needs you.

Many thanks to my classmates at Taos Toolbox and especially to instructors Nancy Kress and Walter Jon Williams for helping me hone this story into its best possible form. I'm grateful also to Lesley Conner and Jason Sizemore of Apex Publications for originally publishing this story, and to Steven Radecki and the team at Water Dragon Publishing for giving it new life in this stand-alone edition. For better or worse, it's every bit as relevant today as it was when I wrote it in 2018.

Finally, all my thanks and love to Nathan, whose support has never wavered.

CHOOSE YOUR TRUTH

T HERE HAD BEEN AN UPTICK IN TRUTH.
Alia's bosses at Prosperity didn't expect her to watch the newstories that filled her queue. Her job was to analyze their local mindshare performance, and watching the content only slowed her down. But she watched, anyway. On an encrypted personal connection via her headset, safe from Prosperity's reach, she tagged each newstory with an extra dimension: *true, fake, true. Partially true. Too biased to categorize. Egregiously fake. True.*

Far more true ones than usual.

Shockingly, true. She lingered over this particular video, frowning, then glanced up and down the long, antiseptic-white office to make sure none of her coworkers was paying attention to her. They were all heads-down at their own screens. She turned back to the offending newstory.

Three times she watched the execution. A familiar, silver-haired figure stood in the center of a bare concrete room, holding an axe. A real axe, real steel; Alia could tell, though Production had given it an extra gleam to draw the eye. This was the radical called the Fist. They led a faction that called itself Choose Truth, though every other faction called it Control. Three times she listened while the Fist condemned a citizen for daring to share content that Choose Truth — that Control — had declared contraband. Three times she watched the axe fall, watched the head wobble across the floor before coming to a stop, empty eyes gazing beyond the camera, away from the spreading crimson. A gruesome, old-fashioned punishment, the commentator noted with barely-contained outrage: fitting for an old-fashioned, ruthless, authoritarian faction like Control.

It can't be true, Alia thought, but she had no evidence to back that up, nothing beyond the feeling of wrongness in her gut, that crawling, uncomfortable sensation that kept getting worse, not better. Gut feelings could mislead, and she knew better than to trust them. *True, true, true. It shouldn't be true. But if it is, people need to know.*

However many times she watched, she found no signs of fabrication in the footage; nothing worse than light editing and editorializing. She dug her fingers into her hair, forcing herself to breathe.

True, she decided at last, and with a pang as blunt and final as that axe blow, she pushed the data point out to her network.

The next newstory cycled up on her screen, and the next, and she no longer watched them. If she reduced the stories to data points and performance metrics, they couldn't touch her.

The borders of her console flared orange, jerking back her attention. She hadn't realized she'd been staring into space. Careless. She could get censured, if someone noticed. All around the office, analysts shoved their active projects aside to respond to the alert, and so did she. A competitor newstory, one that denounced Prosperity, was gaining mindshare at an alarming rate — and it came from Control.

She had to pull herself together and help coordinate Prosperity's response.

•   •   •

Bex knew it would be a bad day the moment the elevator docked and let her into the office. The broad viviglass windows were tinted dark, today, with multicolored graphs and ever-updating mindshare numbers scrolling across, dimming the view of the clouds around them, hiding the grimy city below. The lights overhead emanated that particular blue-white blaze that was supposed to be optimal for inducing creativity under stress, but at this brightness, it made Bex's brain hurt.

Her coworkers debated in tense undertones as they converged on the conference room. The prospect of a meeting cheered her — there were usually pastries at morning briefings — but couldn't overcome the aura of alarm throughout the office.

"What's happened?" she asked her boss, Russhel, as he passed.

He waved at the wall, and her eyes finally focused on the lines that danced across the display. Most of the colors ticked up and down incrementally. Normal stuff.

A couple, including Guardian's electric green, edged upward, which wasn't good. But one line, gleaming gold, dropped like a hacked aircar.

Five points. A five-point drop, overnight, put Prosperity below Guardian, below the Salazar Imperium, below Apiary and even Optimal Frontiers. In one night, they'd lost their lead in mindshare.

"Oh, shit."

"No kidding," Russhel said. "Get to the briefing and pay close attention. The execs are counting on us for idea-gen on countermeasures." He lowered his voice to a kind, conspiratorial tone. "Crisis means opportunity, Bex. I know you've got big ambitions in this place. Anyone who contributes to pulling us out of this mess, even an intern, will get noticed."

"Thanks, boss." She smiled politely. He liked when she called him boss and made him feel like he wasn't at the bottom of the department hierarchy. Was this weird little pep talk about boosting his ego? Or was he actually trying to be supportive?

It wasn't until he'd dashed off that a third possibility occurred to her: the situation was so bad that they would take ideas from anyone. Even her.

•   •   •

Alia struggled to organize her thoughts while she waited for staff to gather. Usually it was easy to keep the narratives straight in her head, but not today. The ideation team interns descended on the tray of pastries, eager to supplement their daily ration bars, and Alia wished the permanent staff would dig in, too. If they were eating, they wouldn't pay as much attention to her briefing.

She set a croissant on her own plate, for show, but didn't eat. She never broke bread with her Prosperity coworkers if she could help it, and didn't think she could choke down a bite of the flaky pastry. Her throat was so dry.

She couldn't afford to make mistakes, not even in a briefing of the junior ideation staff. *Control is aligned with Guardian,* she reminded herself. *This newstory supports Guardian's narrative. That's our analysis. That's all that matters.* Not a silver-haired rebel and a spreading pool of blood. She banished the images from her mind as she would if they were fake, even though they weren't fake.

"You've all heard about today's threat," she began, and the room fell quiet. "It's a low-production, implicit-narrative video depicting violent action by Prosperity against a group of striking factory workers at the tier-one factory in Bethesda. An unusually bold narrative, even for Choose — ah, for Control, who released it."

Get it together, Alia. Focus. She'd never felt this off-balance at the office before. Any other day, she'd have gone home to wait until she calmed down rather than risk making mistakes, but that wasn't an option today.

Alia couldn't show them the video of Prosperity security applying electroshock after electroshock in wide beams against their striking workers, waiting until they struggled to their feet before initiating the next burst. She couldn't reveal that she'd watched it herself. Only the Narrative Analysis team had the conditioning to watch oppositional content without damaging effect, and her role was supposed to be limited to infoflow analysis. She didn't need to see this newstory to analyze how it spread, like the Ephresian flu in a slum in high summer.

She'd wanted to join Narrative Analysis, originally, but Lumi hadn't approved. They'd worried about how the conditioning might interact with her curator training — a gift too valuable to risk.

It had been a valid concern.

"I heard the production quality is really low, like, appallingly low," someone said. "It sounds like an unsubtle hack job. Why would Guardian back content like that?"

"And why would anyone share some piece of low-res inflammatory garbage?" asked one of the supervisors with overwhelming authority, as if he knew any more about it than the others. "It breaks all the rules of narrative conveyance."

"It's low-res because of —" Alia caught herself, heart pounding in her ears. She'd been about to say, *because of the distance, it's hard to get quality footage from a rooftop a kilometer away.* This was bad. She shouldn't be here. She needed space to get herself together. "Because, we think, they're experimenting with new narrative design theories." She glanced at her notes to make quite sure she had the right language. "Reviving archaic tactics with a new spin. Consumers are used to highly-produced videos. This is something new, and consumers share what's new."

"They've stolen an awful lot of our mindshare for Guardian, and a chunk for themselves, too," the supervisor grumbled.

"Yes, and the next mindshare rebalancing is only a few days away," Alia said. A few days before power was redistributed and each faction gained or lost control based on its share of the public consciousness. If nothing changed, Prosperity would lose ground badly. "That's why Prosperity is counting on you. The leadership wants to win back what we've lost by any means possible. Any idea will be considered, so long as it aligns with our central narratives. We need to show consumers that Prosperity is the right faction for them." She ran through a list of the narratives that Analysis considered best for the task.

"And what about Control? How do we stop the Fist?"

Against her will, the clip invaded her memory again: silver hair, a flash of steel, pools of blood in a deep, undoctored red. True, when it shouldn't, couldn't be true. *Lumi, how could you? That's not what we do.*

Nausea warred with a deeper, fiercer anger born of betrayal. She swallowed hard.

"Keep up what you've been doing to turn the consumers against them," Alia said. "It's working."

•   •   •

Bex hung back as her teammates shuffled out of the meeting room, waiting for Alia to finish a conversation with another ideator. She snagged an extra Danish while she waited, wrapped it in a napkin, and licked the jelly off her fingers. If she scored enough free food, she could save part of today's ration bar and trade it to one of her roommates for a few days off chores.

The conversation ended, and the analyst headed for the door. "Um, Alia?" Bex called.

Alia jumped, startled. "Bex! Sorry, I didn't realize you were waiting for me."

"Are you okay?"

All through the meeting, Alia had kept tripping over her words, deviating from narrative in subtle ways that made Bex uncomfortable. Now she was jumping at nothing. People slipped all the time, but Alia never did. Alia was brilliant, always precise, always articulate. Sometimes, in meetings, Bex made notes about the things Alia did that made her seem so together because maybe some were things Bex could learn to do, too. But today, Alia was all jittery.

"Yeah, yeah, I'm fine." Alia flashed a strained smile. "Just distracted, that's all, like everyone is today. What's up?"

Bex took a deep breath. "So, I'm guessing you probably don't have time to meet today?" Alia had promised to walk through the metrics on Bex's last couple newstories with her, to help her understand how infoflow analysis worked. It had been on their calendars for two weeks.

"Oh, no, is that today?" Alia's gaze went distant as she checked her calendar on her headset, and she grimaced. "What bad timing. You're right, we'll have to reschedule. Can you send me a new invite? I'm sorry, I know you've been waiting for this."

"It's all right." Bex thought angry thoughts at Control for picking today to release this particular newstory. "I really appreciate you taking the time for it."

"Of course. And in the meantime, we've both got work to do. Russhel will be looking for your best work today."

She was right, and Bex tried to console herself with that. Prosperity needed brilliant ideas to reverse the mindshare loss. Why shouldn't one of them be hers?

•　　•　　•

Back at her workstation, Bex summoned a list of projects in progress. All the obvious responses were already underway: calming statements by celebrities with high trust quotients, interviews with factory workers proclaiming their support for Prosperity, clips showing Prosperity's good deeds in Bethesda and here in their headquarters-city of Prospera.

That was all damage control. To get their mindshare back above Guardian's before the rebalancing, they'd need a big surge, a counter-attack. That was where the Ideation team came in. Bex dove into generating the best ideas she could, and for most of the day, she forgot about her suspicions.

But by day's end, with the storyboards for her top concepts sent off to Russhel, she found herself sitting near Alia in a cross-department review of a batch of response newstories. An intern's job in meetings like this was to be quiet and pay attention — and that meant she could watch Alia, too.

"That's great work," Russhel said in his obnoxious, I'm-an-expert voice. This newstory showed a food delivery drop right here in Prospera, part of Prosperity's massive new campaign to counteract food shortages in its territories. They were past the point of talking about food being plentiful — they'd lost that narrative battle because you could only push consumers' beliefs so far, even among Prosperity's own loyalists. Instead, they'd pivoted, showing their generous response to the crisis while pinning the blame on Guardian's interference with open trade. "See there? Just a touch of tears, suggesting the depth of her relief. Nice."

"And it does double duty, narratively," said Alia. "For anyone who remembers when Prosperity released that over-engineered pesticide and caused massive crop failures, it makes them look good to be providing food for so many."

"Yes, that story was a nasty narrative move by Control," Russhel said with a frown.

Alia flinched, as if she'd caught herself in a mistake. "Yeah, it was. Really nasty," she said, but she didn't sound appropriately bitter. She *sounded,* Bex thought, like someone who'd been listening to oppositional narratives.

A spy? It can't be, not Alia. It was a horrible thing to accuse someone of, but every staffer was trained to look for the signs. Alia sat there so stiffly, looking so unhappy, and she'd been slipping up a lot. A chill ran through Bex. *Please don't be.*

"It's more impressive how they cleaned up Jubilation Square," said one of the junior staff, and everyone chuckled. Production had done an amazing job of showing smiling locals picnicking on actual green grass in front of the iconic, gleaming monument.

Bex let the video draw her attention back, the way it was designed to. Smiling workers in Consumer Services uniforms sharper and newer than anything the real Consumer Services department could afford. Boxes of food so large that families worked together to carry them off to groundcars or the train. A close-up of a five-year-old boy, sneaking a tomato out of a box and taking a big bite, at which his mother laughed instead of scolding him as juice dripped down his chin. The boy looked like Bex's niece, same wispy, black baby hair, same grin. Same love of tomatoes.

This was good work from a top faction. Bex was lucky to be here, today, in this office, where someday she might get good enough to make newstories like that.

She owed a lot to Prosperity for this internship. If someone in the mid-ranks might be a spy against her faction, she couldn't ignore that. And if that person had been friendly to Bex, taught her, even mentored her, and had been a traitor this whole time, then Bex wanted to be the one to turn her in.

But she had to be sure. So, when Alia peeled away at the meeting's end and disappeared into the bathroom, Bex kept an eye on the door, waiting to see her come out. And waited. And waited. The longer she waited, the uglier her suspicions got.

At last, impatient, she headed for the bathroom herself. As she reached it, the door swung open, slamming into her. She leapt back with a startled cry.

"Excuse me!" Alia said as she came out and saw Bex. "They should put a sensor on this door, huh?" It was the right thing to say, the same quip other women in the office made whenever they had a near-collision, but Alia didn't make eye contact, and she headed, not back to her desk, but toward the elevator, tapping out a message to her headset with agitated jabs of her fingers.

Bex grabbed her coat and followed.

•   •   •

The message had come in the middle of a meeting, leaving Alia distracted and miserable anew: "We need to talk. Now."

Lumi knew better than to contact Alia during shift. And Alia did not want to talk to Lumi right now. Didn't think she could manage it politely.

I know what you did. I saw the video, and it was true, true, true. If it was fake, she'd have known.

She ignored her messages for the rest of the meeting, like a good, obedient mid-level Prosperity staffer, and when the meeting ended, she ducked into the bathroom, the only place in the office with real privacy. A follow-up was waiting for her.

"Not kidding, Ali," the message read. "You've been compromised. I'll meet you at the usual place."

Alia pressed her head back against the cool wall tiles, raised her eyes to the harsh overhead lights. She'd thought she would have more time before she had to confront Lumi about the things she'd seen. She could go home to her closet apartment and sleep on what to do, or at least, she could lie awake on her lumpy bed, refusing to shut her eyes, trying not to see the blood ...

No. When Lumi called, Alia came. It was why she'd gotten into this hellish position in the first place. That wouldn't change, not until she got some answers.

Leaving the bathroom, she ran headlong into an intern, which startled her so badly it could only confirm her decision. She had to get out of here.

"On my way," she sent, and with a swelling dread, she headed for their meeting spot.

•   •   •

The elevator carried them down through the glowing clouds, into the gloom of the city below. Bex merged with the crowds of workers heading home, sticking close enough not to lose Alia amid the masses of protesters that always waited outside the newservice entrance. A mass of Prosperity loyalists chanted their demands for greater action against Guardian to end the food shortage, while scattered pockets from other factions shouted at the departing Prosperity workers, accusing them of made-up wrongs from their own factions' attack stories. It was a relief to descend into the quiet of the rail station. She slipped into a train right behind Alia and stood with her face toward the door. She shouldn't have worried. No one ever noticed the intern.

"Jubilation Square," the train announced a few minutes later in its ever-cheerful voice, and the taste of tomatoes flooded her mouth. *Jubilation Square.* It was awfully tempting to go see the food drop in person. If she was lucky, Alia would get off here. Or if her chase ended up revealing nothing, she could come back before they closed and get a tomato or two. She wanted to see her niece with juice dripping down her chin like that grinning boy in the vid.

A few people got off, but not many. They must not have seen the newstory. She started searching for the story to share it to the train's local feed, until someone nudged her aside with a mumbled, "Excuse me."

It was Alia. Luck was with her; Bex could actually see the drop without losing her quarry, and could swing back to pick up a box afterward.

Drawing breath in anticipation, she climbed the stairs out of the underground and faced the dismal scene of Jubilation Square.

The bleak familiarity bludgeoned her. She stopped where she stood, disoriented, while passengers shouldered her aside from the station exit. The dissonance was too much: in place of the shining monuments and green turf that stuck in her head from the video, she faced dingy gray streets and a pigeon-stained obelisk rising from a circle of churned brown muck.

And there were no boxes. No delivery center, temporary or otherwise. No sign of any drop-off at all.

"Where is it?" she whispered.

"Where's what?" asked an old man who was taking shelter from the rain in the station entrance.

"The food drop."

Even as the words passed her lips, the answer clicked into place in her brain. Disappointment gripped her, a deeper, sicker feeling than the hunger in her gut: disappointment, not in the feed, but in herself.

That creative team should get a prize. Like Russhel said, damn good work. Really believable.

The newstory was so well done that she'd let herself get swept up in it. She'd forgotten it was a newstory. And that was the whole *point,* they were designed to get into your head, seep into your memories, to make you believe in the narrative with your whole being. That was how narratives lived and grew, carried by their stories. The more a faction's narrative stuck with consumers, the more mindshare they gained, and this was a Prosperity narrative. She should be *glad* it had worked so well. She should be messaging back to the office, a rueful joke about how this newstory was so good she'd forgotten it was one of theirs.

She shouldn't feel betrayed by her own faction's narrative.

"No food drop here today. You should check your feed," the old man said helpfully. "The last one was a few weeks back. Real good one, I heard."

Of course, he wouldn't have seen the newstory; it was targeted at non-local markets, outside Prospera, where no one would suffer the same cognitive dissonance she had. In a couple days, they'd release a new, local version, vague on the details of when the drop took place, so locals could share the video around and commiserate about how they'd missed it. It would be distant enough by then that everyone could let themselves believe it was real. The "last one" this man thought he remembered wasn't any more real than this one.

"I'm sure it was great," she muttered.

"Maybe you'll catch the next one," he said.

With a jolt, she remembered the actual reason she was here. Where had Alia gone? Damn it, if her moping over a too-good newstory had cost her best chance to catch a spy in the act ...

Feeling wretched, she stepped out into the rain, ignoring its sting against her cheeks as she scanned the crowd.

There! A woman, head bowed under a gray rain-suit indistinguishable from all the others, but there was a familiar tightness in her gait. Bex deployed her own rain-suit, a cracked and plasticky old model that was nevertheless better than the rain's burning, and dashed across the square, soaking her shoes in murky puddles in her haste to catch up. At the corner of an adjoining street, her quarry paused and looked around. Bex ducked, pretending to adjust her rain-suit settings. It was definitely Alia. *Making sure no one's following you? Now why would you need to do that?*

Bex ghosted down the street after Alia, who slipped into an abandoned bar off a narrow, trash-filled alley. It was a good place for a covert meeting: far enough from downtown that there were few cameras, and far enough from the really bad neighborhoods that Safety didn't keep much presence here. Avoiding the smelliest puddles, Bex knelt in a spot just outside the bar, sheltered behind the half-wall where she could watch through a broken window without being seen, and waited.

"Hello, Alia."

Bex startled along with Alia at the voice. Someone was standing behind the bar, which had been empty a moment before. They threw back their hood, and the dim light glowed off silver hair.

Bex stifled a cry of alarm. She would recognize that silver hair anywhere. She blinked-captured a few images and sent an urgent, private beacon to the nearest Prosperity Safety office, attaching the photos and her location.

This was the Fist. The ruthless leader of Control, who wanted to overturn the rule of narrative mindshare and tell people what content they could see.

And Alia — brilliant, shining Alia — was their spy.

•　　　•　　　•

"You came." The familiar, smoky voice made Alia's stomach twist harder. "I'm glad. I wasn't sure you would."

"I wasn't sure, either, but you owe me answers."

"For what?" Lumi cocked their head, leaning against the grimy surface of the pitted wooden bar, as if waiting to pour non-existent bourbon into the smashed remains of glass tumblers. The two of them used to drink old-fashioneds together, here, tucked into the smallest corner table. That was at the beginning, back when mingled chatter of anonymous after-work crowds was enough to give their conversations privacy. The meeting place had stuck, but now, only ghosts made of dust and cobwebs remained. Only dim, gray light reached inside, deepening Lumi's brown skin into shadows, leaving nothing of their expression visible below their crown of short, spiky silver.

Body language spoke clearly enough, though. They were going to make Alia speak her accusations aloud.

This was the same Lumi she'd always known, and it was impossible to imagine them doing ... *that.* But it was also the exact same Lumi from those videos, the Fist with their signature silver hair and custom-made, gunmetal smart-jacket. The pleased smile they'd given her when Alia agreed to go undercover, mirroring the smirk they wore in the video as they swung the axe.

"You ... you killed those people. Why?" She could barely choke out the question. "That's not what we do."

A pained look crossed Lumi's face, a deeper shadow in the gloom. "No, it's not. It's *not.* Ali, they got to you."

"I saw the video, and it was *true* ..."

"They fooled you. That's why I'm pulling you out." Lumi reached for her shoulders. Alia swatted their hands away, stumbled sideways into a stool. Broken glass ground under her heel, and Lumi stopped. "Those videos of me, they were fakes. Manufactured, like ninety-six percent of everything Prosperity puts out."

"They were real. I should know." That was why Choose Truth valued her so: Alia could sift the truth from

17

the falseness in the factions' narratives, tagging them so anyone who cared could avoid the false and stop their eyes from lying to their brains. She was the best curator Choose Truth had, and she was never wrong.

"I think *I* should know if I'd gruesomely murdered a bunch of innocents." A smirk flashed, brief and bitter, then faded into grimness. "That's what tipped us off. Prosperity has a new way of fabricating content that curators can't detect, and we didn't even know it until they started faking stories about us. I'd hoped you might see through it, but when you flagged that video today as true … I figured otherwise."

She drew a deep, trembling breath, and trained all her attention, all her skill, on Lumi. "Say it. If you didn't do it, say so straight out."

Lumi's gaze latched onto her, utterly serious. "I did not kill a citizen with an axe. I have never killed a person in my life."

No hint of a lie. No falseness in the face, the voice, the eyes. It was one thing that made Lumi so good at spreading the truth: they'd always been a terrible liar.

The breath rushed out of her, and Alia fumbled for the stool. Lumi took her arm to help her, and this time, she didn't pull away. Her skills, her training, useless. A newstory could lie to her as easily as anyone else. It was hard enough to keep narrative from taking over your world when you *knew* it was false, and now, if there was no certain way to tell …

This had to be how most people felt all the time. Adrift, deceived. Lumi came around the bar and slid onto a neighboring stool, waiting in supportive silence while she processed the news. Alia sighed. "We'll have to find a way around it and update the trainings. The basic trainings should still be okay, but at the advanced levels ... it'll take months, and until then, we can't approve anything the factions put out. Is it just Prosperity? Or other factions, too?"

"Prosperity may not know, yet, what they've stumbled upon. But I've got warrior-journalists in six factions' territories working to verify or debunk the latest stories our curators have flagged as true."

"The mindshare rebalancing ..."

"Doesn't matter. I'm worried about the long game, not who wins or loses power this week. People are finally starting to see why our work matters. If we have to stop —"

Lumi whirled and aimed a light from their jacket sleeve at the broken-out windows. Alia hadn't heard a thing, but Lumi's enhanced hearing was eerily good.

"Who's there? Come out, slowly."

"We won't hurt you," Alia added, remembering the cruelty on Lumi's face. *That was fake. The real Lumi doesn't hurt people.*

A figure rose outside the window, hesitated, then marched through the open doorway: a girl in a cracked rain-suit. She put back her hood, revealing an expression of disgust. "You traitor. You've been with them this whole time."

"Bex." Alia sighed. "A Prosperity intern. She must have followed me," she told Lumi.

"What do you want to do about her?" Lumi asked in a low voice.

Alia's infiltration was over, so it didn't matter if the kid blew her cover. And Bex was young, not yet on the inside at Prosperity. Alia hated making hasty judgments about people based on gut instinct: her gut could lie, and she hadn't decided yet what to think about Bex. But she needed to decide, right now.

"She's a smart kid. Observant," she murmured, and Lumi nodded in understanding.

Let's see if she's got good sense, too.

•   •   •

"Okay, Bex," the spy said. "You're right, I work with Choose Truth. But the narratives you've heard about us, they're lies meant to discredit us. It's not what we do."

"All the narratives?" Bex shook her head, clinging to her sense of betrayal. *I'm not an idiot. You can't fool me, anymore.* "The factions don't agree on anything, but they all have the same narrative about you."

The Fist smiled. "That's because we don't have a narrative. All we have is the truth, and that threatens all the factions equally. They're scared shitless of us."

"Of course, you have a narrative. Everyone has one."

"Narrative is *all* most factions have," Alia said. "They put narrative at the center of everything they make. We center the truth."

Truth. An obsolete word, like "nation" or "vote," long since declined into irrelevancy. A word that might have meant something in ancient times, when information was hard to come by, but now, narrative was necessary to create meaning and purpose from a flood of data. Narrative was everything. "What's the point?"

"The point is stories you could have watched with your own eyes, if you were there. Raw, undoctored footage. That's what we create, and on the rare occasions when the factions put out true stories, curators like Alia promote it as such."

"But that factory strike video …"

"Some of my best work. Not easy to get, that footage," the Fist said smugly. "I camped for three days on a rooftop within the security zone with an ultra-zoom lens."

"You were actually there?" The wildness of traveling hundreds of miles to get footage for a newstory that could have been produced in the most basic studio made her brain stall for a moment.

"That's far from the greatest lengths my warriors have gone to, in order to capture true stories."

"See? You say you've got no narrative, but you call yourselves warriors." She shook her head. "You talk about truth, but you tell people what they can and can't watch. There's a reason everyone calls you Control."

"That's not —" Alia burst out.

The Fist waved her silent and leaned forward, voice lowered confidentially. "Have you ever actually watched Choose Truth's feeds, Bex?" Bex had to shake her head. "So, you believe whatever Prosperity says about us. That's comfortable, isn't it? It's nice to listen to your preferred faction. You ingest the narratives that match your beliefs, that show you the type of world you want to live in, and ignore the rest. When a mindshare rebalancing comes around, you give factions power, not based on what they do for you, but what they say. Even if it's all lies."

"But it's our choice! We have the right to decide what narrative we want to live in. You can't force people —"

"All we do is give people the option, the *choice*, to tell the lies apart from the truth. To live based on more than a tidy, comfortable narrative. Many people want that. And for people like you, who don't care what's true, we won't interfere."

"Or maybe not like you," said Alia. "I've seen you at work. Have you never been troubled by a newstory you knew was pure fabrication? Never got frustrated that Prosperity's narrative is so distant from your actual life?"

"No. I like Prosperity's narrative." But Bex could smell those tomatoes. It had shaken her, the contrast between that green, bountiful narrative and the bleak reality of Jubilation Square.

But she didn't blame Prosperity. That computer-generated kid was damn cute, optimally cute, designed for maximum mindshare, and yet … *It would have been a nice thing for us, if it was true. I would have liked to taste that tomato.*

Talking about bounty was much easier than providing bounty, but the narratives only went so far when she crawled into bed hungry, waiting for the next day's ration bar.

A creak as Alia twisted on the old bar stool, watching with half her attention while one hand tapped out a command to her headset. The rain had stopped, but the sun hadn't returned yet, and water from the eaves dripped dully onto the pavement outside. The Fist considered Bex with a too-perceptive gaze, like one of the jays in Golden Park, when it thought you had food. Their eyes were silver, too, nano-enhanced. Who knew what they could see?

"You're mad at them," the Fist said. So gentle that it was unnerving. She'd watched them commit such violent acts, scenes that, true or not, had taken root in her brain. "It's okay to be mad. You can —"

Bex didn't hear a thing, but the Fist's gaze snapped toward the window. Then came the pounding of booted feet in the alley. Lots of feet.

Alia tensed. The Fist sighed and rolled their eyes as an amplified voice called, "Stand down! We're bringing you in for questioning."

Safety swarmed into the room, a dozen officers, armed with electroshock guns. A file transfer request pinged in the corner of Bex's vision — a local, line-of-sight transfer — and it startled her so that she accepted it without thinking. But it wasn't from Safety, it was from —

The Fist flung a coin-sized object onto the floor, and Alia shoved Bex in the opposite direction. Bex dropped and kept her head down as electroshock beams crackled in the air. The Fist grabbed Alia and dove for the bar, just as the coin exploded into a blinding burst of blue light. More wild shots, but Bex couldn't see a thing. She lay still, blinking spots from her eyes.

When she could see again, the Fist and Alia were gone.

Officers converged on the bar, weapons trained, but no one was there.

"A trapdoor! It's sealed."

"Blow it and follow them!" the commander shouted. "And search for other access points!" That was the work of minutes. Soon, all the officers had vanished in pursuit except for two, who approached Bex.

"You're the one who called in the sighting? Prosperity appreciates your loyalty, miss. We have to ask you some questions."

"And we'll need any data you have from your encounter with the terrorists."

That new file glowed in her incoming queue. A big file, multi-modal, labeled Truth Curators Training Level One. Before she could think better of it, Bex buried it in her personal files.

"Of course," she said. "Whatever you need."

•　　•　　•

Bex didn't see the end of the chase. Safety led her off before she found out whether Alia and the Fist were captured or escaped. The questioning was mild, mostly focused on whether Bex had been infected with Control's ideas. It wasn't hard to satisfy them.

She turned over all her recordings of the incident, but the file, she kept hidden. She thought daily about how it would be better, safer, to delete it, but despite every logical reason, she didn't.

•　　•　　•

"Look, we've got some good ones today!" Russhel effused.

The latest batch of Prosperity newstories was out, released to staff a few minutes before it hit the live feeds. Bex skimmed through them. He was right, the production team was on its game today. They'd done a smash job with her dog-befriends-rat idea, and ...

Before her hovered corpses. Two bodies sprawled across a sea of wrecked concrete and bent rebar. Two heads, one dark, one silver.

She choked, an ugly cough racking her entire body. Doubling over, she couldn't block out the image that now filled her head, the bent limbs and bloody jacket.

"You okay?" Russhel asked with apparent concern.

Recovering from the cough gave her space to recover her thoughts, to orient her mind to this new narrative. "Yeah. Sorry, got startled by the bodies, the ..." What was Prosperity calling them? Terrorists. To Prosperity, Alia and her friend were terrorists. "... the terrorists. Wasn't expecting that."

"That whole incident must have been disturbing for you. You did good work, leading Safety to them. I don't know how we would have gotten our mindshare back up before the rebalancing without this!" His grin dimmed. "It's a shame we couldn't bring them to trial, though."

"Yeah, a real shame." That was what Russhel expected to hear.

Bex made herself watch the whole story. It said Prosperity had captured Control's leaders, thanks to a tip from a loyal consumer, and had learned they'd planned an attack on Prosperity Newservice headquarters. An attack against a faction's newservice was an attack against the freedom of narrative, against the freedom of all people everywhere to consume content as they chose. Fortunately, with the two leaders in custody, Prosperity's hard-working, elite security forces foiled the plot long before it reached fruition.

Most unfortunately, the leaders were killed while attempting to escape.

No.

Bex shut off the video. Beyond her screen, charts on the walls showed this newstory creeping upwards in the mindshare rankings. She needed something blank to look at, something narrative-neutral, so she shut her eyes, and held, side by side, two contradictory stories.

Choose Truth was a group of heroic rebels, warriors offering people freedom from the faction narrative machine and its lies.

Control was an authoritarian regime, set on destroying people's hard-won freedom to base their reality around the narratives they preferred.

Alia, alive.

Alia, dead.

Both stories couldn't be true. She'd called their notions about truth obsolete, but this, she needed to know. This *mattered.* It *mattered* whether Alia was honest, whether the Fist was right. Prosperity's newest narrative was already extending its tendrils into her thoughts and memories, pushing out the things she'd seen with her own eyes and replacing them with claims of wrongdoing and those still, horrible bodies.

In a newstory, a corpse was easy to fabricate.

If Prosperity was lying and they were alive, hiding, planning their next move, then maybe Prosperity was lying about Choose Truth's intentions, too. And if they were dead, if Alia was dead, there was one less curator in the world. One less person who could see through the lies and elevate the truth.

Bex had claimed truth didn't matter, but with the difference between Alia alive and Alia dead … it mattered.

She sat forward in her chair, shaking. For the dozenth time, she read the text that had accompanied the file, a set of canned instructions, followed by a hasty, personal note:

> *I know the lies bother you, no matter what you pretend. Our advanced trainings need updating,*

but this one will get you started for now. Won't teach you everything, but the basics should still work. Hope it helps.

If her boss discovered this program, she'd lose more than her job, and it might not even give her answers. Prosperity had learned to fool even Alia, and this was just beginner stuff. Such a risk for such a slim chance ...

But it was a start. She opened the program and ran it.

Alia's voice emerged. "This is a Choose Truth training program for recognizing fake and manipulated content. Welcome to lesson one."

ABOUT THE AUTHOR

Jo Miles writes optimistic science fiction and fantasy. Their short fiction has appeared in numerous places, including *Lightspeed*, *The Magazine of Fantasy & Science Fiction*, *Analog*, and *Fireside*. Jo is a graduate of the Viable Paradise and Taos Toolbox writers' workshops, and their story "The Longest Season in the Garden of the Tea Fish" in *Strange Horizons* was nominated for a WSFA Small Press Award.

Jo lives in Maryland, where they help nonprofits use the internet to save the world, but mostly serve the whims of their two cats. You can find them online at *jomiles.com* and on Twitter as *@josmiles*.

YOU MIGHT ALSO ENJOY

BEST SERVED COLD
by Bob Schoonover

A dish of corporate greed served with a side of revenge.

BUSINESS CARDS
by Laureen Hudson

This story encompasses five jobs, four managers, and a shocking number of actual occurrences and people. And if you recognize yourself here, well ... I'm sorry about what happened next, but I was on assignment ...

REDUCTION IN FORCE
by Steve Soult

A heartless corporate layoff leaves Gil Schaffer emotionally shattered. A revolutionary memory erasure procedure may be his only hope for salvation, but the price could be greater than he bargained for.

CPSIA information can be obtained
at www.ICGtesting.com
Printed in the USA
BVHW080024010323
659387BV00007B/363